To the voters of the future, remaking this country for the better.
—AD

To Deven, Ava, Teagan, Mia, and Taylor, who inspire me to work hard to leave a better world for them.
—RB

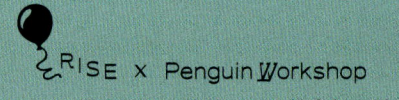

An imprint of Penguin Random House LLC, New York

First published in the United States of America by Rise × Penguin Workshop, an imprint of Penguin Random House LLC, New York, 2024

Text copyright © 2024 by LFS Touring, Inc.
Illustrations copyright © 2024 by Rachelle Baker

Penguin supports copyright. Copyright fuels creativity, encourages diverse voices, promotes free speech, and creates a vibrant culture. Thank you for buying an authorized edition of this book and for complying with copyright laws by not reproducing, scanning, or distributing any part of it in any form without permission. You are supporting writers and allowing Penguin to continue to publish books for every reader.

PENGUIN is a registered trademark and PENGUIN WORKSHOP is a trademark of Penguin Books Ltd. The W and RISE Balloon colophons are registered trademarks of Penguin Random House LLC.

Visit us online at penguinrandomhouse.com.

Library of Congress Cataloging-in-Publication Data is available.

Manufactured in China

ISBN 9780593383773   10 9 8 7 6 5 4 3 2 1 HH

The text is set in ABC Ginto Normal.
The art was created with Procreate, and iPad, and unknowable cups of hot tea.

Edited by Cecily Kaiser
Art directed by Maria Elias
Designed by Meagan Bennett

SHOW UP AND VOTE

by Ani Di Franco

art by Rachelle Baker

RISE
NEW YORK

i learned what it meant to show up and vote

it was a nasty november, windy and raining

and in that book

she found my mom's name!

mama signed her name again
right next to it

i said

it made me feel proud
that i figured something out
and i felt proud to be there
helping my mom

then i got excited when we got invited

it seemed special and secret
that no one could see us
i felt kind of nervous
but mama looked calm

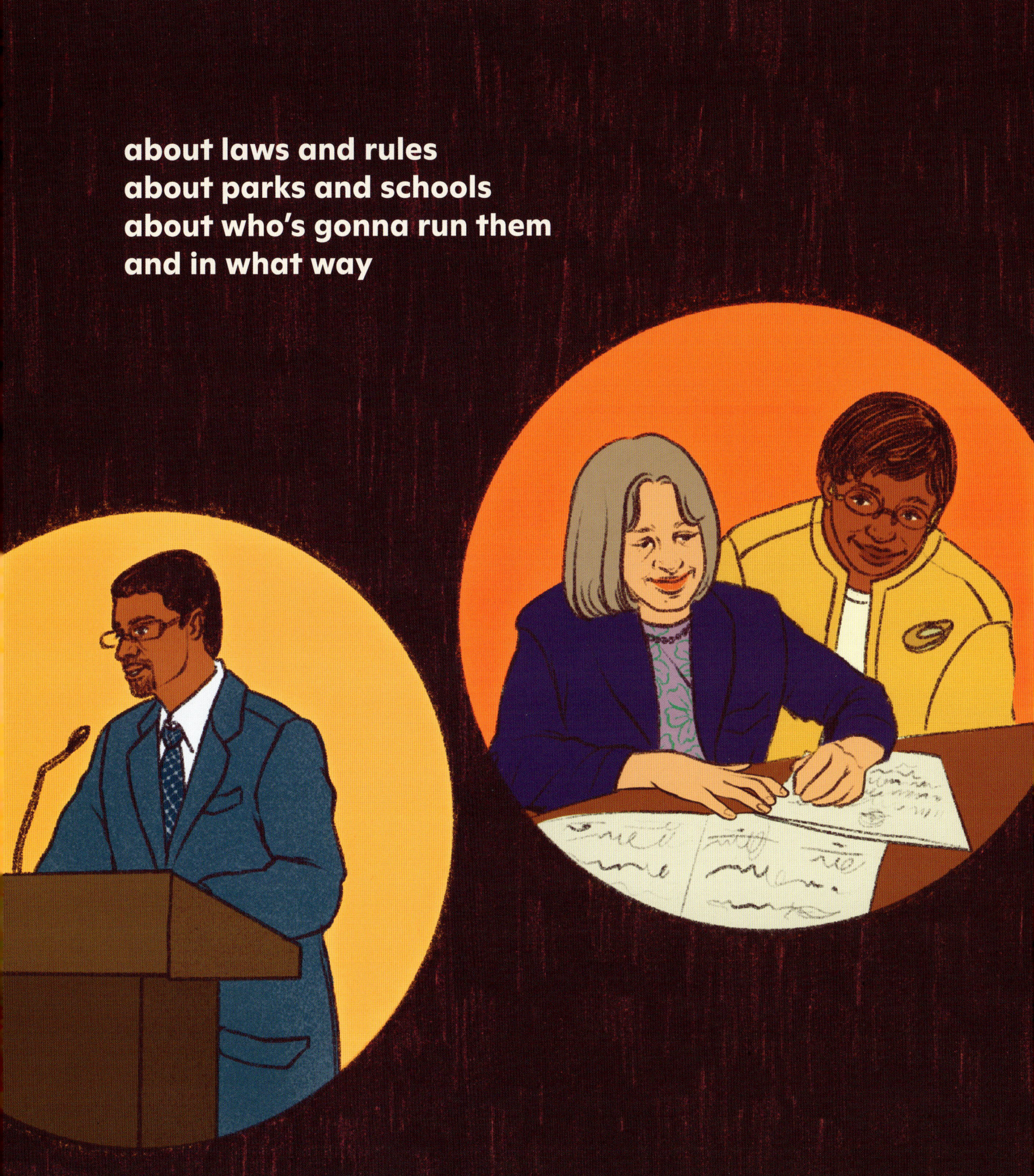

then she chose the names
and i pushed the buttons
and each little button
lighted a light

before the last button
mama paused and said

and on our way home
i looked all around

the same things were there
but i saw a lot more

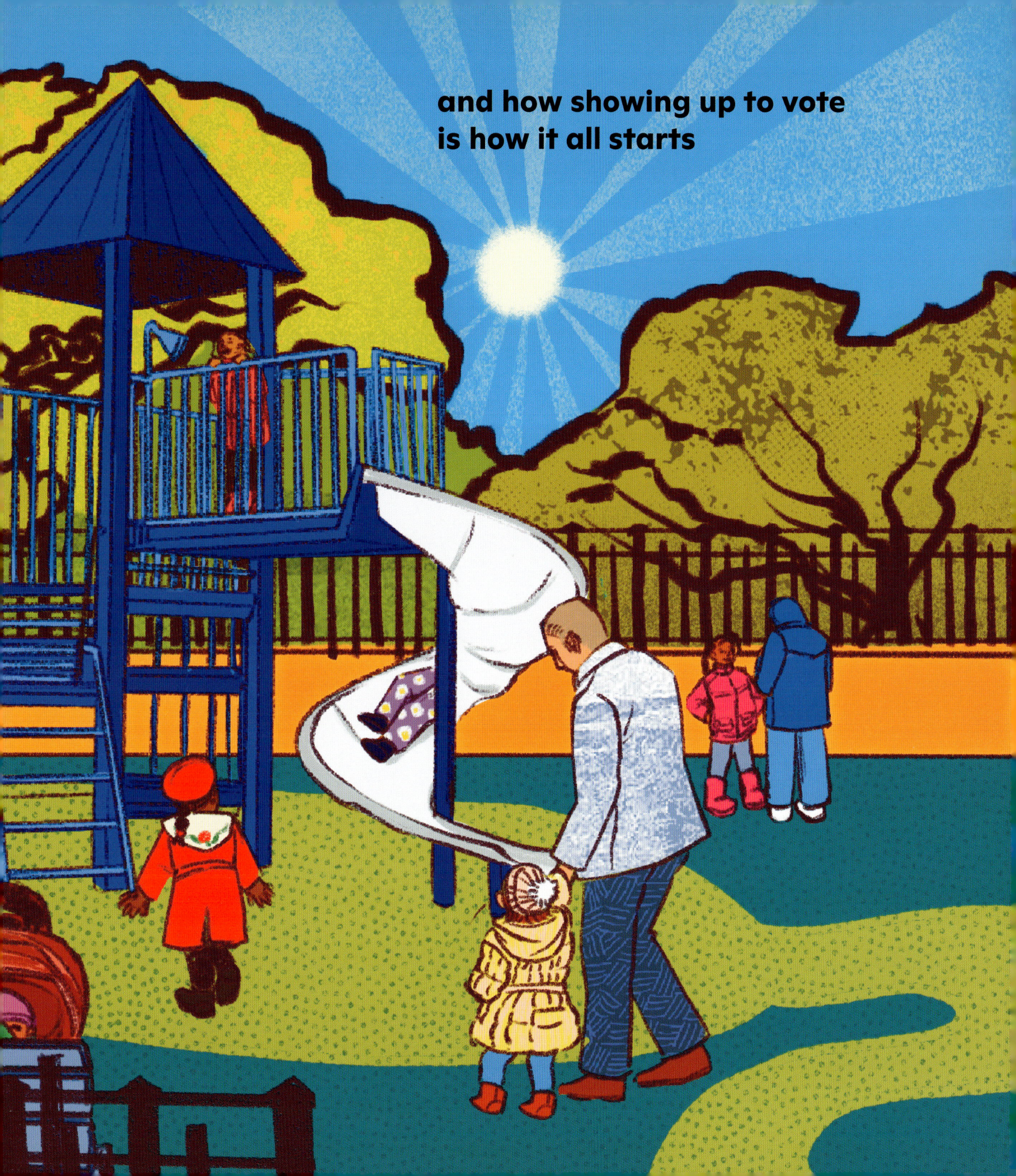